FAITH over FEAR

Written by: Paige N. Hampton
Illustrated by: Danielle N. Seago

IN MEMORY OF

Faith Marie Hartzell, who never gave up, never gave in and always gave her all.

And to all the other little princes and princesses fighting a dragon: always keep the

FAITH.

ONCE UPON A TIME...

there was a beautiful little princess named Faith. She had a smile so bright and a heart so big that no one could help from falling in love with her and wanting to be her best friend.

Not only was she the most beautiful princess anyone had ever seen—with her hot pink hair and bright blue eyes, but she was also the most fun-loving princess to ever exist.

However, Faith was no ordinary princess. Oh no, Princess Faith was also a superhero! This happens to be very helpful when you're a princess, especially with possible dragons trying to work their way into your kingdom.

♥

As a matter of fact, one day, a mean, nasty dragon came and tried to get Faith, but she wasn't even scared! She found a sword and made up her mind that she would beat that dragon, and she did!

Not only did she beat it, but she also created an army so big she couldn't be stopped. An army so faithful and so devoted that they would never leave her side and would do everything in their power to protect her and her kingdom.

So she celebrated her victory with them and went back to enjoying being a beautiful little princess! And of course, when you're a princess and you defeat a dragon, a dance party is always in order, so dance she did!

Princess Faith was enjoying her life and was starting to feel safe again. But then, out of the blue, another mean, nasty dragon tried sneaking back into her kingdom. Now this didn't make Princess Faith very happy. She knew she had to do what any other superhero princess would do, get a bigger sword, create a bigger army, and take that monster out for the second time.

Again, she and her army danced and celebrated! It started to seem that these nasty dragons had gotten the memo once and for all. She again felt safe outside in her kingdom, until the biggest dragon in the land suddenly arrived. Princess Faith had grown tired of fighting dragons and decided she wanted to dance instead.

Since a sword isn't needed to dance, she traded it for a beautiful white ballgown. Her army understood. They knew how difficult being a superhero princess must be. Princess Faith decided to go inside her castle to dance from now on so as not to be bothered by any more pesky dragons. You see, Princess Faith's castle is a perfect, safe, and beautiful place.

In her castle she needs only to dance. She has no worries, her song is always perfect, and she is as carefree as a princess should be. One day, she will welcome her faithful army into her castle for the most magical dance party anyone has ever seen! Then we'll all live happily ever after with our princess, FAITH.♡

ABOUT FAITH

On Christmas eve in 2011, at age 6, Faith was diagnosed with a cancerous tumor on her spine. After almost 15 months of being cancer free, she was again diagnosed with a secondary leukemia.

Faith always fought hard to battle her "dragons" and built an army of faithful supporters along the way. Her journey on earth ended on March 30, 2015 after a courageous battle, but her story still lives on in those who love her. ♥

Made in the USA
Lexington, KY
21 October 2018